My Friend John

by Charlotte Zolotow

Pictures by Ben Shecter

Harper & Row, Publishers · New York, Evanston, and London

E

for Ursula and Mary
with love

I know everything about John

and he knows everything about me.

We know where the secret places are

in each other's house,

and that my mother cooks better

but his father tells funnier jokes.

ice cold
LeMonede
4¢aGlass

COlD
ORANGEADE
1 9lASSfOr 4¢
2 9lASSES fOR
9¢

He can't spell   and I can't multiply

10

so we help each other.

11

His mother
won't let him out
if the weather's bad

but I can come over
in any weather,
even if it's pouring rain

or windy

or a blizzard.

We always stick together

because I'm good at fights,

but John's the only one
besides my family
who knows I sleep
with my light on at night.

He can jump from the high diving board

but I know he's afraid of cats.

I hate orange juice

and John won't eat any ice cream
unless it's chocolate.

I know where he keeps the things
in his bureau drawers

and he knows what's in all the closets
at my house.

He saw me cry once

and the day he broke his arm
I ran home and got his mother for him.

25

We know what's in each other's refrigerator,

which steps creak on each other's stairs,

and how to get into each other's house

if the door is locked.

29

if the door is locked.

I know who he really likes

and he knows about Mary too.

John is my best friend
and I'm his

and everything that's important about each other we like.